My Friend Ben and the Sleepover

Charles Beyl

Albert Whitman & Company
Chicago, Illinois

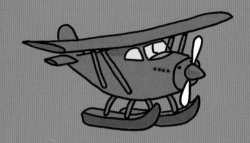

This book is dedicated to my Oakbrook friends
and the wonderful time we spent outdoors.

Library of Congress Cataloging-in-Publication data is on file with the publisher.

Text and illustrations copyright © 2021 by Charles Beyl
First published in the United States of America in 2021 by Albert Whitman & Company

ISBN 978-0-8075-5309-1 (hardcover)
ISBN 978-0-8075-5312-1 (ebook)

Printed in China
10 9 8 7 6 5 4 3 2 1 WKT 26 25 24 23 22 21

Design by Aphelandra

For more information about Albert Whitman & Company,
visit our website at www.albertwhitman.com.

I'm Chip, and this is my friend Ben.

Ben asks if I want to have a sleepover.

I've never slept anywhere but home before.

Ben is so excited.

He says we can
build a fort and
sleep in it.

We can shine
flashlights
when it's dark.

We can tell spooky stories under a big blanket.

I want to go. It sounds so fun!

I pack my backpack with my pajamas and my toothbrush.

Mom adds some fern snacks, apple leaves, and a fresh branch to nibble on.

Ben's mom picks us up.

Mom and Dad wave goodbye.

My house looks smaller as we go.

So do Mom and Dad.

Ben's house is big.
The logs and sticks are
higher than the ones at our house.

Ben and I run to build our sleepover fort.

We build high towers,
sturdy walls,
and a secret place to sleep.

Ben finds a blanket to hang over the towers.

Ben has an airplane that floats.

I miss my toys.

I wonder if Mom and Dad are playing with them right now.

We play inside our fort
until it starts to get dark.

We have roasted acorns and
a big twig salad for dinner.

We always have fern-and-bark casserole
at home. But this tastes good too.
Dad would like this dinner.

We take flashlights to our fort.

We can shine our lights almost to the stars.

We crawl into our sleeping bags. It's cozy.

Ben tells a spooky story about a ghost.

I tell one about a monster.

I think the shadows near the woods look a little like ghosts. Ben thinks the rocks look like monsters.

Maybe we should go inside.

We listen to the night noises.

Crickets, frogs, and...

OO!

Ben and I run fast under the ferns, around the stumps, and over the rocks to the door of his house.

Ben shines his flashlight into the dark.

It was just Mrs. Owl!

I was scared.

Ben was scared too.

It's better to be scared together.

We spend the rest of the night
in Ben's room.

I can't wait for our next sleepover.